Naughty Stalker

Zoey Zane

Cover Design by Elle Berlin

Author Logo Design by Tanya Baikie – More Than Words Graphic Design

Editing by Rachelle – R. A. Wright Editing

Proofreading by Dee – Dee's Notes Editing

Formatting by Rachelle – R. A. Wright Editing

Dedication

For the ones with mask kinks.

Epigraph

There is no excellent beauty, that hath not some strangeness in the proportion.

— Francis Bacon ("Of Beauty")

Fair Warning

Naughty Stalker is a dark and spicy novella. Reader discretion is advised. TW for stalking, stepsiblings, exhibitionism, and mentions of cheating (not main characters).

Chapter One

Madi

"DRINK, GIRL." EVIE RAISES my arm, pushing the drink toward my mouth. "You gotta keep up."

I down the rest of the champagne in one gulp, hoping it'll hit my blood quickly. Something needs to soothe these nerves. "Better?"

Instead of speaking, she grabs my glass and places it with hers on a server's tray. The server pauses, and Evie grabs two more, then hands me one.

I bring the glass to my lips and take a small sip. My brain is already foggy, so I set the glass on the ledge beside me. Despite what Evie says, I don't need to keep up.

What I need is to be fucked.

Rode hard and put away wet.

Utterly and thoroughly fucked six ways from Sunday.

Casual, no strings attached, primal sex.

It's just for one night. One night with no inhibitions.

I can do this. And it's about damn time.

Swaying my hips to the music, I lose myself in the beat, dancing with the crowd. The champagne warms my body, the heat spreading down to my toes. The thoughts in my head dim as the music gets louder.

Someone wraps an arm around my waist, pulling me into them. I turn my head and discover a mask obscures my view. Taking a deep breath, I remind myself not to think or analyze. Just do. Just feel.

Our bodies sway in sync, like dancers who have known each other for years. Seemingly able to read my thoughts, he spins me around the floor, weaving us between different couples and leading us in dance. We lock eyes, and a shiver disturbs my soul so great that I'm not sure I'll ever recover. My heart thumps faster with each step, each twirl. When the song ends, I assess my dance partner.

He's dressed in a sleek black suit with a navy-blue tie that matches my midnight-blue floor-length dress surprisingly well. Almost too good, like we coordinated colors for our senior prom.

Everything about this man in front of me screams intense. A wicked smolder flickers in his green eyes before I break our trance to run my gaze up and down his body. I can't see his face behind his Venetian-style mask. His broad shoulders fill out the suit. It's not one that looks rented for the occasion—for as good as it fits, it has to be tailored specifically for his tall stature.

"Thank you for the dance." I smile. "Find me later?"

"Madi!" Evie's voice floats from somewhere behind me.

I turn for a split second, and when I turn back, the mystery man is nowhere to be found. *Dammit.* Glancing around the room for a minute, I shake my head, unable to locate him. He dressed for the occasion and blended in with the crowd. More than one person is wearing a black suit and mask tonight.

It is a Halloween masquerade ball, after all.

"Madi!" Evie motions for me to join her at the bar, then hands me a bottle of water. "Here, finish this. Looks like you need it after that dance."

"You have no idea," I pant, then take a long sip, relishing the cold. "I've never had a dance that powerful before."

"I need a cold shower after watching you." She fans her face dramatically. "But seriously, who was that?"

I shrug. "Didn't think to get his name. It's not like I told him mine either."

Someone knocks into Evie, sending her flying into the bar top. "Hey, watch it!" she yells.

"My bad. May I have this dance, mistress?"

Her eyes widen, and she gasps. "Oooh. Yes, you may." She waves to me as her mystery man pulls her to the dance floor.

The bartender places two tequila shots in front of me. "Your friend," he says, pointing to Evie.

I knock one back, then the other.

Someone taps my shoulder and holds their hand out, silently asking for mine. Before I can accept or decline, they spin around and hurry off in a different direction. I shake my head. *How odd.*

Now, where's my mystery man? Scanning the dance floor doesn't change my luck. I don't see Evie either. I sigh and glance toward the stairs. Maybe she went up there.

Exiting the main room, my heels click on the tile floor as I walk down the narrow hallway. The music from the dance floor plays softly in the background. It's not much of a walk to the stairs. The hallway is covered in fake spiderwebs, with plastic skeletons hanging from the ceiling and orange and purple twinkle-lights creating a path up the stairs. They wrap around the handrails like Christmas garlands.

A bouncer greets me at the top of the stairs. "Hand please," he says, and motions toward the black light.

"Oh, sure." I hold my hand under the black light, and a pumpkin appears.

"You're good. Thank you, ma'am." He unhooks the red rope, allowing me to step through.

I turn the corner, and loud sounds of intimacy fill the large space. A couple of small groups are clustered around the room, performing various sexual acts. It's hard to decipher where one moan ends and another begins. There's so much to take in, but what captures my attention is a bigger group in the left corner. Chains rattle as a woman hangs from the St. Andrew's cross.

Inching closer, I can't take my eyes off the scene. A stunning woman dressed in nothing but high heels and a tiny black thong faces the cross. Her hair is pulled into a low ponytail. Her moans get louder as I get closer, and they say everything she can't. A shirtless, masked man teases her body, dragging a flogger up and down her back before pulling back and aiming for her ass. Her chest heaves as she pants. She turns her head just before the strike lands, and her eyes gloss over as the flogger meets her skin. The chains on the handcuffs rattle against the rings of the cross, her body leaning into the impact of each hit.

"Enjoying the show?" A rough voice hits my ears, causing a clench within my core. We didn't speak the entire time we danced, but I know it's him—my mystery man.

My breath quickens, and heat floods my body. Unable to speak, I nod. He places a hand on my hip and pulls me into him. His hard length presses into my lower back, and I gasp, electrified by his touch. The way my body responds to him is something I've never experienced before, not with anyone.

Feeling bold, I lean back into him more and grind my ass against him. He growls in my ear and whisks me away, taking my hand and leading me into a secluded room to the right.

He flicks on the lights, and a warm glow fills the room as the lock clicks behind him.

"I'm—"

A finger on my lips stops me from finishing my thought, then he walks to a wooden desk on the other side of the room and leans against it. "Come."

Heat pools in my core with each step I take deeper into the room. My gaze roams over his body, and now I know without a doubt. He found me—my mystery man.

I meet his smoldering green eyes, and the same intensity as before greets me. He sweeps his fingers gently across my arm, then places a hand on my shoulder.

"On your knees."

My legs act of their own accord, and I kneel before him. He undoes his belt and pulls down the zipper, unfastening his pants so they fall around his ankles. Then he pulls out his cock.

It's impressive. Thick and veiny. Hard and bouncing when he lets it go. I lean forward to take the tip in my mouth. Closing my eyes, I tease the tip with my tongue before releasing it. I lick my way down his shaft and back up to the top. He groans as I take him in my mouth and suck.

I've never done anything like this before—a blow job in a public place. Sex in a public place. I mean, I know he locked the door, but there are two windows on the opposite side of the room. I don't know if anyone can see me or hear me. I can't find an ounce of care within myself to stop it.

Desire pools in my stomach and threatens to overtake me when he places his hands on either side of my head. The head of his cock hits the back of my throat, and I gag. He holds my head in place as he withdraws, allowing me to catch my breath. Slowly, he slides himself back into my mouth and hits my throat again. And again. And again. Each time I gag, it lets him slide a little further, until his balls hit my chin as he fills my mouth completely. Tears sting my eyes, and I'm so turned on. His movements are measured—every thrust timed perfectly.

Not a moment too soon, he pulls my head off him. I gasp for air, and my breaths come out as pants. He fumbles to open the desk drawer beside him, pulls out a blindfold, then removes my mask and slides it on.

If he doesn't fuck me . . .

My mystery man helps me to my feet and spins me around just as quickly. He pushes my chest into the desk and raises my dress. His hand caresses my ass, then slides in between my legs.

"Say red if you want me to stop," he whispers against my ear.

"Fuck," I whimper when his fingers press inside my opening. My pussy aches. An ache I've never felt before—an itch that will never be scratched.

He groans, pumping his fingers inside me.

"Ah!" There's a sharp sting on my ass and then a sucking motion. *He bit me!* "Oh, fuck." His fingers work magic inside me, and he reaches around with his other hand to play with my clit. He works me over, higher and higher. Then, he removes his fingers, and the warm wetness of his mouth is on me. He licks up and down my slit, pushing his tongue into my pussy.

Stars flutter across my vision, my body tightens, and waves of pleasure flow through me. He greedily accepts my orgasm, slowing down to let me ride it out. My body slacks against the desk, spent.

A wrapper crinkles behind me, and before I have a chance to recover, he slides into me.

"Yesss," I moan.

He nudges my right foot. I spread my legs a little wider, and he pushes my leg up with his knee to rest on the desk. His cock penetrates me at an angle I didn't know was possible.

"Fuck . . . Yes . . ." I chant. His thrusts become erratic with no rhythm. He fucks me wildly before slowing his movements. "Don't stop," I plead. "Please."

"You're taking my cock so good," he whispers.

His voice lights the fire inside me, sending my body into another orgasm.

"That's it," he says. "My little dove." A moment later, his cock twitches. He pumps into me once more, then stills. He kisses the nape of my neck before pulling out.

I lie sprawled on the desk while I catch my breath, my body tingling like every strand of hair is standing on edge. He tugs my dress back down, gets dressed, opens the door, and then all is silent. I tear off the blindfold and realize he's disappeared into the darkness without saying a word. My heart flutters like a bird getting used to its wings. What an adrenaline rush.

One night of sex with a stranger . . . Who knew it would feel so fucking exhilarating?

Chapter Two

Madi

A WEEK AGO, I wouldn't have thought I'd have the spine to sleep with someone I'd never met. It's refreshing, especially after years of being told to stand in the background and let someone else shine.

Blake wasn't a terrible boyfriend. He just did what jerks do: cheat and blame the other party. She came on to him; it was an accident—he fell, and her pussy caught him. When he wasn't cheating, he pushed me behind him, ensuring I didn't outshine his success. Not that I ever wanted to, nor would I ever do so, but he's the epitome of only-child syndrome. I wanted to be his equal, not his second place.

"Cater to me, I'm first, service me. Me, me, me." *Barf.*

Finding out he was cheating was honestly the best thing that could have happened. I'd been looking for a way out but couldn't muster up the courage. Sure, I invested a couple of years of my life with the man-child, but we needed to move on. Evie told me all along he'd never put my needs first. I was naive to think he would, even knowing I can't change someone who doesn't want to change. My mom taught me to always look for the good in everyone.

Last night was out of character for me and wasn't at the same time. I'm *not* the person to have one-night stands or sex outside of relationships. My sexual palate is a little daring and devious—one that Blake wouldn't appreciate. He was strictly a missionary-position man. Sadly, I had to fake more orgasms than not.

Still, when Evie suggested I attend the masquerade Halloween party with her, I initially declined, stating I needed to be more desperate to look for something. I'll never forget her response.

"Desperate? Oh, honey. If you're desperate, you sign up for a dating site. You go to the masked club because it's invite only and with like-minded people. You're safe there."

She's not wrong. You can only get into the club through an invitation from someone who's already a member. Thankfully, Evie was gracious enough to extend the invite. The thought of having sex in front of others—or even near others—sends a chill of arousal through my body.

Blake would've never embraced something of that nature—filthy, thrilling, forbidden. I needed more than he could give me, so I wasn't devastated when he cheated. It was a sense of relief more than anything.

The more I thought about Evie's suggestion, the more I realized it was time for my needs to be met. It's time to put myself first, and holy shit, I'm so glad I did! Regardless of my hangover headache, last night was the best night of my life. Sex with a total stranger in a locked room with darkened windows, where people may or may not have seen or heard us. One night where names weren't exchanged but the orgasms were plentiful. The champagne I consumed before the two shots helped soothe my nerves and allowed me to get out of my head. Once I stopped thinking and let myself be in the moment, everything was stripped away, and I found what I craved.

Evie and I got together last night and crashed at her place. Coming home at two in the morning, drunk and freshly fucked? I didn't dare face my mom. She has a nose like a bloodhound, and I'd rather she stays out of my sex life.

"Good morning, gorgeous!" Evie's cheerful disposition is not what I want this morning. She opens the blinds in the living room, and I pull the blanket over my face.

"Go away," I groan.

She whips the blanket away from me and presses something cold against my arm. "Sounds like you definitely need this. Take it."

I squint at Evie, sit up, and mindlessly reach out. She places two small pills in my hand and hands me a bottle of water with the other. I uncap it, toss the pills in my mouth, and take a big drink. "Ah, thank you. Now turn down the lights."

"You can't turn down the sunlight."

"Easy, close the blinds," I protest, leaning my head against the back of the couch.

A few minutes later, the nutty aroma of Evie's favorite coffee enters the living room. I rub my eyes, then wildly glance around the room. No Evie. *Dammit.*

Pulling my long brown hair into a messy ponytail, I sigh. "Evie?"

No answer. Begrudgingly, I stand up and walk toward the kitchen.

"Evie, I swear to God, if the coffee is not ready . . ."

Evie's leaning against the sink, giggling at something on her phone. Two cups of coffee sit on the counter, one much lighter than the other. I roll my eyes and pick up the darker cup. I like my coffee like I like my nail polish—black with no fuss.

"Mmm," I groan as the coffee hits my tastebuds. "Perfect as always."

Evie smiles and slides next to me, lightly bumping my shoulder. "So, last night . . . Something you'd do again?"

"In a heartbeat." I don't even pause to think about it.

"You, an exhibitionist? Never would've guessed," Evie teases.

"Last night was . . . mind blowing. Not just sex with a stranger, but the atmosphere and everything. There was no shame, no hiding, no guilt. Just pleasurable sex."

"I told you." Evie laughs and picks up her coffee, then takes a long sip. "It's not usually like that every time you go. The attire, I mean."

"It should be." I sigh. "There's something about dressing up for a ball and getting railed on a desk by a random person."

She gasps. "On a desk? You little devil!"

"It was so good. Like made-my-toes-curl good." My cheeks flush, remembering the way the mystery man took me.

I'm nowhere near ready to start dating again, but it would be good to have a little fun . . . Fun that is about three years overdue.

She places her mug in the sink and says, "Want a ride home before I head to work?"

"Work? On a Saturday? What are you, crazy?" Yes, she is. Evie is the co-owner of Home Sweet Home Antiques. She's one of the best owners I know.

"Inventory weekend," she says with a laugh.

"A ride would be awesome, thanks." I place my mug next to hers in the sink. "So, about this giggling I walked in on . . . Who's the guy?"

She tells me about Luke, the stunning tall drink of water who bumped into her last night. He moved to Crimson six months ago and hardly knows anyone outside his coworkers. They spent the remainder of the night dancing, drinking, and making out in a dark corner as though they were back in high school. I haven't seen Evie smitten with someone in a long time—at least since graduation, which was six years ago.

Luke's taking her to this fancy place on the outskirts of town tomorrow night. We've been wanting to try the new restaurant, but it's booked out for the next three months. Apparently, he has connections. I'm impressed so far, but he didn't share with Evie who his connection is.

Evie switches the conversation to her store, and as much as I try to pay attention, my mind drifts back to the mystery man. I needed that more than I realized. I needed *him* more than I realized, and I don't even know who he is. He was in tune with my body and played me like a fiddle. Whether it was because it'd been a while since my last orgasm or what, I'm not sure. Either way, I want it again.

I *need* it again.

We turn onto my street, and I immediately notice something's off. Evie slows down and pulls up next to my car in the driveway. Without speaking, I climb out of the passenger seat, walk to my car, and pick up the package. Sitting on the hood of my emerald Taurus is a bundle of orange and black balloons tied to a small glass car filled with orange M&M's.

"Who's that from?"

I jump at Evie's voice. "I don't know."

There's a card taped to the bottom. Careful not to rip it, I unstick it and hand the container to Evie. Sliding my fingers into the envelope, I pull out a white index card with two pumpkins stamped on the front. I raise my brows as I turn the rectangle over:

I'll see you soon. X

Chapter Three

Madi

THERE SHE IS—STANDING AT the end of the bar, looking cute as fuck in her faded tank top and shorts that look like somebody ripped them from a pair of jeans. What's funny is that she doesn't even realize the effect she has on people. She's five feet, one inch tall, with long dark-brown hair and blue eyes that pierce your soul. What she doesn't have in height, she more than makes up for in sarcasm. She steals my breath away. Slowly but all at once, my whole world changes.

"Madison Montgomery! Maxi Mad. Mad. Are you mad, Madi?" I holler just loud enough over the music so she can hear me, then take a few steps toward her until I'm right behind her.

"You must have a death wish!" She whips around and runs straight into my chest. Her eyes narrow as she realizes it's me. "Of fucking course you do. No one calls me that anymore, Declan."

"What? Maxi Madi? I bet I could get everyone to start again," I tease, smirking when her face turns red.

"I see how much you've changed. Fuck you," Madi huffs.

I wink. "Anytime, sweetheart."

She shakes her head, her cheeks turning from red to bright pink. "Ugh, you're such an asshole!"

"At least I'm not Ms. Goody Two-shoes."

Watching her get riled up is a thrill each and every time. My dick stirs in my pants as I remember how close I was to her asshole last night. Never in a million years would I have imagined finding my little dove in the masked club, ready to fuck anyone who walked up to her.

"You need an off button," Madi retorts.

"Madi, drinks are ready." Evie sneaks up behind me and shoulder checks me before grabbing their drinks.

I chuckle and move out of her way. "Nice one, Evie."

"Oh, I didn't see you there." She shrugs and turns to Madi. "You ready, girl?"

"Yes, please." Madi nods and takes a sip of the drink Evie handed her. The two of them lock fingers, then weave their way through the small crowd at the bar.

I grab my drink from the bartender and spin around to lean against the wall closest to the bar. It's the best vantage point for viewing the dance floor. Madi's hips sway in beat to the music, and my thoughts drift back to last night's dance.

Her fiery look is now burned into my brain. I've seen various sides of Madi through the years, but I don't think I've ever seen her like that before. So carefree and wild. It's intoxicating. The way her hips moved was similar to how they are now. Her body instinctively leaned against mine when I held her close, almost as though it knew she was mine.

Under the disguise of a mask, I felt comfortable enough to approach her. If I had known how much I'd be hooked, I would've done it a lot sooner—*years* sooner. Hell, I would've made her mine the moment she turned eighteen, and I never would've let her go, fuck the consequences. Instead, I've been patient, biding my time until the moment is right.

The moment I heard her voice and realized who the woman in the midnight-blue dress was, it was over. I've always watched her from the shadows, even when we were younger. Seeing Madi in a wanton place like that turned me possessive. She's such a good girl, prude-like and seemingly untouched. She was not leaving the club without a small taste of the forbidden. A taste of me—something most would object to. I need my little dove to crave me as much as I covet her.

After our dance, someone in a phantom mask approached her at the bar. I walked toward her, hidden in the shadows, and cocked my head to the side at him. Instead of taking her hand to dance, he immediately walked away. I smirked, knowing I wouldn't let anyone get close to her.

Eventually, Evie disappeared on the dance floor with someone and left Madi unattended. She was safe there, sure, but not from me. I followed Madi up the stairs and watched in fascination when she surveyed the room before her. My dick hardened as I took notice of everything her body was doing. Her chest heaved a little faster with her breaths, and she leaned forward a little, like she was imagining the impact of the flogger against *her* ass rather than the naked woman's. I crept up behind her and noticed her cheeks burned a bright red. It was all I could do not to remove my mask and kiss her neck.

Back in the room, I took a risk when I removed my mask. Thankfully, she complied with the blindfold. She's born to be mine and only mine. Her hot mouth on me wasn't enough. I *had* to taste her, to suck on her sweet pussy, to feel her orgasm in my mouth. The moment her orgasm hit my tongue, a force of pure primal instinct overtook me, and now, one fuck is not enough. One of anything with Madi will never be enough, but I have to let her come around to the idea of us being together before I start filling her up with my cum.

Madi's sultry voice interrupts my thoughts. "Take a picture. It'll last longer." I clear my throat and shift my hips away from her, hiding the raging hard-on that hasn't quit since last night. "She is single, you know."

"Who, Evie?"

"Not that I'd want you fucking my best friend, but yes. She's interested in someone right now, so you better act fast," Madi teases.

"No thanks. I'm good." *Evie's not the one who has my attention.*

"Your loss." She smirks. "Now, why aren't you out gallivanting around spending your daddy's precious money? I hadn't heard you were home."

Much to her dismay, after I graduated from high school, I took a gap year and traveled the country before finally settling into college for my degree. It was a tension point between my dad and me. I wanted a year off; he wanted me to start college. We compromised—I'd take a year off, then take additional classes to catch up for my missed year. Then, after I completed undergrad, I'd come home and work for his architecture firm. Growing up, I found what my dad did for a living fascinating. He'd design buildings and help bring them to life. The city courthouse is actually one of my dad's designs. It's our little secret that I picked out a few permanent things about the courthouse—very few people know the window arches and glass were my ideas.

Madi and I were close when we were younger, but then I left for the gap year, and we drifted apart. I traveled, experienced many things, left my life behind, and she was still here, finishing her senior year in high school. She stayed after graduation, attending the local university and interning at Crimson's interior design firm.

And now I'm home. I've come back for my little dove. My Madi.

"Wouldn't you like to know?" I wink at her as I drink in her essence, committing it to memory so that when all goes to hell, I'll still remember what she smells like. Cinnamon and apples. So fucking good, like drinking apple cider on a cold fall night.

Without thinking, I reach up to push some of her fallen hair behind her ear. She gasps at my touch and shakes her head, stepping back. I love how responsive she is. The gasp draws my attention to her slightly parted red lips, begging to be kissed and bitten.

I bite my lip to stifle a groan. A moment later, Evie shoulder checks me again.

"Do you have a problem?" I ask. It doesn't surprise me—she's hated me for the last eight years—but it is rather annoying. She flashes me a wide grin and hands a bottle of water to Madi.

"Nope, as long as you stay out of my way."

Madi suppresses a laugh, then downs half of the bottle. She puts the cap back on and shoves it into my hands. "Since no one wants to dance with you, hold my water."

I take the bottle and watch her lead Evie back to the dance floor.

It's getting harder and harder to resist the urge to tell her, to kiss her lips and claim what's rightfully mine.

Mark my words—she will be mine. I will burn down anything that stands in my way.

Chapter Four

Madi

I FLIP TO THE next page of the design book and growl in frustration. For the first time, an interior decorating project isn't consuming me. Hannah wants her new home to be decorated like her personality: bright and bubbly. Usually, I have no issues finding a starting point for the project. This time, though, it's hard to concentrate and make the client's vision come alive.

And it's all due to the masquerade ball.

"Need some help?" Evie sits in the chair beside me and digs out the book with various floral arrangements.

Shaking my head, I turn the page again. "No, but thanks. I don't know what I'm doing right now. I can't focus." I close the book and toss it back on top of the pile.

"Okay, you've been zoning out all week. What's going on?"

I turn to face her, a blush creeping up my face. "I think I saw him yesterday."

"Saw who?" She eyes me curiously.

"The mystery man from the other night. It had to have been him." The look on her face gives me pause. "Now, I know what you're thinking, but hear me out . . . I was at the home goods store trying to find inspiration for this project. I'm the only one in the back of the store when I feel it—a shift in the air. I turn down the aisle, and there he is. He's dressed in plain clothes but wears the same mask."

"What did you do?" Evie squeals.

"Nothing. I mean, what was I supposed to do? Walk up to him and ask him if he's the one that fucked me so good I can't stop dreaming about it?"

Her eyes light up. "Yes, that's exactly what you do!"

"I'm not you, Evie." I grab a couple of M&M's from the bowl in front of me and pop them in my mouth. "Besides, I'd die if he had no idea who I am. There's no way it was him."

"Do you know anything about him? Anything at all?"

"No. He barely said thirty words to me the whole time. It's not like I was begging for a conversation."

His eyes, though. There's something different yet familiar about them. Like I've seen them before—like I've spent my whole life looking into them. Maybe it feels that way because I feel so drawn to him. My body has never reacted this way before, not even with Blake. It's unreal, this connection between us.

"You could try going back. Maybe you'll run into him again?" Evie suggests. "I mean, he's intent on seeing you again. Find him instead." She grabs a couple of my M&M's to emphasize prove her point.

"Yeah, maybe." I pick the design book back up and flip through the pages again. It isn't a bad idea, honestly. The page in front of me is covered in yellows and oranges, filling me with a sense of enlightenment. All at once, the client's vision comes together, and I decide to seek out my mystery man.

I quickly enter the club, a cold October breeze nipping at my toes. Getting in is much easier than last time. The bouncer scans my ID, stamps an invisible ghost on my hand, and waves me through.

The club pulses with a kaleidoscope of flashing lights tonight, casting a different glow than the twinkle lights on the night of the ball. After I grab a drink at the bar, I lazily walk around the room, soaking everything in. I'm in no rush; I know he'll be here. Various couples are dancing close, swaying to the beat. Hardly anyone wears masks tonight, and I'm not surprised I don't see anyone I know. Outside of Evie, the people I surround myself with aren't the club-going types. They're more the staying-in-playing-games family types—which isn't bad; it's just not my cup of tea all the time. I finish my drink and set the glass down on the bar.

"May I have this dance?"

I turn around and come face-to-face with Tristian. So much for not knowing anyone here. Tristian had a crush on me throughout high school. Sadly, knowing I had a thing for Blake didn't stop him from hitting on me any chance he got. I've skillfully avoided him over the years.

"Sure, Tristian." I smile.

He leads us to the center of the floor and places both hands on my hips, leaving me to wrap my arms around his neck. We move slowly, even though the speakers aren't playing a slow song. His blond hair falls over his forehead, and his lips curl into an appreciative smile, captivated by something. I blink a few times, but when I turn my attention back to him, his eyes fill with hunger, a hunger I cannot fulfill.

We're halfway through the dance when my whole body tingles with awareness. It's like an invisible thread wound around me, pulling at my instincts and drawing my attention to it. A shiver traces down my spine, a whisper of intuition that will not be ignored.

My heart thumps faster as I spin us around, picking up the pace. And then, as if guided by the invisible thread, I tear my eyes away from Tristian and peer into the darkness across the room. *He's here, stalking me from the shadows*. A silhouette stands tall in the dimly lit corner with a mask covering his face. A breath catches in my throat, and heat pools in my belly. Our charged connection comes to a head when our eyes lock. I remove my hands from Tristian's neck and thank him for the dance. My feet act of their own accord and propel me toward my mystery man, each step deliberate, like a moth to a flame. A sense of vulnerability and anticipation fills me, an intoxicating mixture.

As I draw closer to him, my heart pounds faster. "I've been waiting for you." He holds my gaze with a knowing depth of secrets and unspoken desires. A daring thrill courses through my veins, urging me further into the magnetic pull.

He holds his hand, and I greedily take it, closing the distance between us. Without hesitation, he leads us up the stairs, where the bouncer scans our hands before letting us through the roped area.

We barely reach the main room before his hands are all over me. His touch sends an eclectic jolt through my body, every point of contact igniting a trail of fire between us. I lean into his embrace, trailing my fingers along the nape of his neck. His fingers dig into my flesh, eliciting a loud moan from my lips.

"No peeking." His voice is rough in my ear.

Everything in me complies with his demand. I squeeze my eyes shut and tighten my grip on his neck, waiting.

He plants the softest of kisses on my lips, and the feeling of his lips on mine is gone before the kiss sinks in. I whimper, and he chuckles. Hands still planted on my hips, he guides us to a corner, then turns me around to face the wall. A cold silk cloth wraps around my head, ensuring I couldn't see him even if I tried. He hitches up my flowy red dress and caresses my ass before biting the soft spot between my neck and shoulder. He slowly hooks his fingers into my panties, slides them down my legs, then helps me step out of them.

"Mine," he growls, his voice tight and low. He nips at my neck, lifts my dress again, and slowly pushes a finger inside me. "So wet . . ."

My core clenches around his finger, and I moan when he adds another one. "Yes," I breathe. I push my ass toward him, needing him. He slowly pumps his fingers in and out of me, then picks up the pace. "Oh, fuck."

"Look at you soaking my fingers."

My heart sings with his praise. I can't believe how turned on I am right now. My arousal fills the air around us, and I'm close to the edge. He laces his other hand through my hair and pulls the strands in his fist. His lips touch my neck, and before I can help it, I fall apart in his grip. He holds my hair tighter and lets me ride out my orgasm on his fingers. All the other noise in the room ceases to exist—it's just me and him.

"That's it," he says, withdrawing his fingers once my orgasm subsides.

"More," I whisper. The word falls from me brazenly.

A moment later, the tip of his cock hits my entrance, and he slides in quickly and stills. "If you want more, take it."

My hips buck against him as I move my body against the wall. After a few attempts to find a rhythm, I growl. I need more, and he senses it, pumping his hips to meet mine. His thrusts overtake mine, and I allow myself to feel. To take everything he gives me. The desire for my mystery man consumes me.

He's all I can think about. He's all I need. Even as he pumps his cock in my wet pussy, it's not enough. Within minutes, I'm coming again. My body hums with the pleasure of my orgasm. He kisses my neck and chuckles.

He snakes his hand between my legs and finds my throbbing clit. His fingers strum it as he pumps in and out of me at an unyielding rhythm. I squirm against him and cry out. God, it feels so good.

"Your sounds are dangerously addicting, my little dove." He bites my neck, sucking on the skin so hard I'm sure it'll leave a mark.

My pussy clenches around him, my whole body aching. Between the pressure on my clit and his cock filling me, the waves threaten to overtake me again. It's almost too soon.

"Oh, fuck. Please . . ." I pant.

I freeze, my body on fire, twitching from the sensations of this delicious tryst. White-hot pleasure radiates through me before coming to a boil and sending me spilling over the edge.

A sinister laugh rings in my ear. "Good girl," he groans, and then he stills, falling over the edge himself. He slides out of me and pulls my dress down, then takes my hand and guides me to a sitting position on the couch against the wall. "Wait two minutes before taking off the blindfold." He gently kisses my lips and places something in my hand. Something that does not feel like my panties.

I feel the moment he leaves. The air around me hangs empty, shattering our intimate bubble. The seconds tick by slowly in my head as I count to sixty twice over. Removing the blindfold, I glance down at what's in my hand. It's a small snow globe with a bright red and orange phoenix.

Chapter Five

Madi

A WEEK LATER...

I review my side notes while Hannah finishes flipping through the stack of color swatches on the table. Her hair is golden blond, matching the sun as it pours through the large bay windows of my office. Hannah laughs, then looks up at me with an eager smile.

We've been discussing the vision for Hannah's new house. Hannah and I grew up together and sat side-by-side in most classes. My last name is Montgomery, and hers is Monroe. It's easy to become quick friends when teachers always seat you together. Of course, getting in trouble because you talk too much is just as easy. Hannah's family moved away after fifth grade, then moved back just before freshman year—the first year our teachers randomly assigned seats.

"So, Hannah." I lean forward slightly. "I've reviewed your preferences and additional notes, along with the overall aesthetic you're going for. From our discussions, you're drawn to vibrant, energetic colors. Yellows and oranges in particular, right?"

She nods enthusiastically, her bright-blue eyes lighting up. "Absolutely! I want the space to feel lively and full of energy. My momma always says yellow is my best color, but I need more than just one color, you know?"

My creative wheels turn, and the rest of the vision comes together. "I completely understand, and we'll definitely achieve the vibe you're looking for. Now, let's dive into some specifics. We can consider shades of yellow and oranges to create depth and vision interest. For example, a soft buttery yellow for the walls in the living room, paired with bold orange accents—throw pillows, artwork, and maybe even a statement rug to pull it together."

Hannah taps her fingers thoughtfully on the swatches as she considers my suggestion. "I love the idea of a buttery yellow backdrop. It'll feel warm and welcoming with the bold orange accents. The contrast would pop, leaving me feeling energized. Yes, that'll definitely work."

My eyes light up with excitement. "Great! And to balance out the vibrancy, we can incorporate neutral tones like whites and creams or maybe some light grays. These neutrals will help create a sense of balance and allow the yellows and oranges to shine even more."

She nods in agreement. "Yes, neutrals will keep things from feeling overwhelming. And I've always loved the idea of having lots of natural light, so the combination of those colors and the light sounds like it would work perfectly."

I pull out my tablet and open the portfolio for the design company. Turning it toward Hannah, I bring up pictures similar to the living space I had in mind. Each example exudes a distinct personality and charm, and a mixture of the first two would be a perfect fit for her.

"Another idea is to bring in patterns and textures that play off the yellows and oranges. Maybe a geometric pattern on the throw pillows, or a textured wallpaper in the dining area. Mixing these together can create depth and keep it from feeling dull."

Her eyes linger on the images, and she nods. "I love the idea of mixing it up. It adds an extra dimension to it. Plus, geometric shapes are a modern touch."

"Exactly what I was thinking." I smile, glad to know we're on the same page. "Now, we can go with pieces with clean lines and simple silhouettes for the furniture. This allows the colors and patterns to take center stage. How do you feel about incorporating some midcentury modern pieces? They tend to work best with this kind of color palette."

"Oh, absolutely. I've always loved the midcentury modern style. It's sleek and timeless. Plus, it sounds like it'll complement the look we're going for." She bounces in her chair with excitement.

"To tie it all together, we can bring in some greenery with potted plants or even botanical-themed artwork. If you're like me and can't keep them alive, succulents or extremely low-maintenance plants would be perfect. It'll keep the room inviting and cozy with a refreshing touch of nature." I write a few more notes in my notebook.

"Perfect! I love plants. I actually have sort of a green thumb."

The next couple of hours fly by as we dive deeper into the concepts and plan which products to buy. Hannah's adventurous and outgoing personality and her ability to embrace bold choices make the prospect of designing her new home all the more thrilling.

Our vision takes form and soon represents what her home will look like. As we near the end of our meeting, I can't help but feel a surge of inspiration. "Hannah, I have to say, your enthusiasm is contagious. I'm genuinely excited to bring this to life with you and create a space that captures your personality and style."

Hannah grins back at me. "Thank you, Madi. I've had so much fun discussing this project with you. I just knew you'd be the perfect person for the job. I really appreciate your expertise and your willingness to bring my ideas to life."

I stand from my seat and extend my hand. "It's my pleasure. Designing a home is a collaborative journey, and I'm happy to be a part of it."

She shakes my hand with a firm grip. "Now, it's time for the fun part. Shopping!"

We laugh, gather our things, and walk out of the building together. She gets in her car and drives away. I open the left passenger door, shove my design books in, and settle into the driver's seat. As I turn the key, something red catches my eye. My eyes widen when it registers someone broke into my car. They didn't take anything, though. Instead, they left my red panties hanging from the rearview mirror.

Chapter Six

Declan

MADISON MONTGOMERY WILL BE my ruin, and I will happily bring down the kingdom with us. I cannot get her out of my mind. Every time her heart pulses under my unwavering gaze, the invisible pull between us draws us closer. My lips curl into a smirk as images of last night replay in my head. The only thing that was missing from it was her kiss. I need her lips on mine, her tongue playing with mine, trying to see who will come out on top. My teeth will sink into her bottom lip, and I'll relish the delicious sounds coming from her mouth.

It's become an obsession. She's become my obsession, weaving a spell around me and drawing me deeper into our sinful web of connection. It's a sin to crave every inch of her wicked curves, and I will greedily go through the gates of hell to make her mine.

I palm my dick to relieve some of the building pressure, not that it helps any. Madi consumes me, and she has no idea who I am. Once she does, she'll fight me, but she'll cave. She's cut my chest open and immersed herself in my veins. It's a sickness. There's no one to save her; she's falling with me. And in the end, I always get what I want.

Madi's laughter rings out through the crisp autumn air as she darts through the towering stalks of the corn maze with Evie hot on her tail. Her wavy brown hair catches the last of the sunlight, and her eyes shine excitedly.

"Girls, wait up!" Evie calls. "We don't want to get lost in here."

Lucy and Sophie, Evie's younger sisters, skip along, their giggles blending with the rustling leaves.

Madi grins. "Lost? Where's your sense of adventure?"

Evie rolls her eyes and catches the girls at the fork. "Okay, here's the deal: you have to stay close. I'll let you pick the way, left or right, but you have to stay where I can see you. Deal?"

Her sisters nod enthusiastically, then exchange glances. They both point in separate directions and dart in said directions.

Both women reach out and grab the girls. "New rule: you have to stay close *and* together," Madi says.

"Fine," they say simultaneously.

The four of them follow the left path as it winds deeper into the maze, the towering corn stalks creating a sense of adventure. I follow closely behind them as they travel off the forged path in ways that defy logic. The girls make a decision at each turn, and I wait patiently for the right moment. The walls of corn create a sense of seclusion, as though the outside world has disappeared entirely.

Loud laughter followed by a frustrated whine stops me in my tracks. I'd been lost in thought; I hadn't realized they arrived at a dead end. Sliding the mask over my face, I take a few steps closer to the corner and wait.

The girls turn around first, then start down the next path, followed by Evie and Madi. Before Madi rounds the corner, I pounce and grab her arm, pulling her backward.

She screams, but I quickly cover her mouth, and when she falls against me a moment later, I remove my hand. It's almost too easy.

"You've been watching me," she whispers, her voice filled with lust. "Who are you?"

I smirk behind the mask. "You can call me Phoenix, my little dove."

Shoving her into the tall, dark stalks behind us, I pull an ear of corn off one of the stalks. Madi grips my left bicep and traces her fingers around the muscle as if committing it to memory, then lifts her fingers to my face and attempts to remove the mask. I grab her arm and spin her around. She squirms, twisting out my grasp, and trips over a fallen stalk. I lunge at her, covering her body with mine, then grab her chin, forcing her to look at me.

"I need to see you," she pants. Her eyes sparkle with desire.

My gaze traces the contours of her face, the play of light and shadow adding to her soft features. Sadly, I shake my head.

"Open." I poke her mouth with the corn. She refuses to open her lips. "Okay, have it your way. Everything is a dildo if you're brave enough." She gasps, parting her lips just enough for me to shove the corn in her mouth. "Good choice."

I shove her pants down, unzip my pants, pull my dick out of the opening, and sink into her without a second thought.

"Oh, fuck . . . My dick fits perfectly in your pussy." Relief floods through my body when her walls tighten around me.

She moans against the corn, sending the sweet, delicious sound straight to my dick. I reach under her shirt and find her nipples hard. *No bra. Hmm* . . . I twist one between my fingers and tug on it. Her muffled moans fill my ears as she bucks her hips. If she keeps this up, I'm going to come.

Our frequent public trysts already have me bursting at the seams, but seeing Madi writhing underneath me is enough to send me into a spiral. I search her face as I move my fingers down to her clit. Her eyes widen at the contact and threaten to roll back into her skull. She frantically nods her head.

I strum her clit and thrust into her over and over. With each thrust, her breath hitches a little higher, her body gets a little more tense. She's so close. Leaning my upper body away from her, I'm ready to pick her up and put her on her knees, but before I can do that, she slips her hand under my shirt and raises it to place her palm against me. *Fuck, I wish she hadn't done that.*

Quickly, I push her hand away and pull my shirt back down. She raises her brows in question; I shake my head in response. Placing one hand on the ground above her shoulder, I wrap my other hand around her neck. Her pulse thumps wildly when she understands my unspoken request. She spreads her legs a little wider, sucking me deeper into her.

"Such a good little dove," I growl, tightening my fingers on her throat. Madi's pussy clenches around me, and within a few thrusts, she's falling apart beneath me. Her body shakes with her orgasm, and before she's done, I find my release, diving further into my obsession.

"Madi!" Evie's voice calls out. "Where'd you go?"

Shit.

I quickly withdraw myself from Madi, tuck my softening cock into my pants, and pull her pants back up. Placing a caressing hand on her cheek, she leans into my touch, and how I wish to kiss the ever-loving shit out of her.

Another time, maybe.

Without a word, I stand, turn, and disappear into the stalks of corn. There's a slight pang in my heart, knowing I'm leaving her behind for the moment, but then the ache dissipates when I remember the gift I left hanging on her rearview mirror the other day.

She can't know it's me.

Not yet.

Chapter Seven

Madi

HOLY FUCKING SHIT. THAT was the hottest thing I've ever experienced, even more so than the last two times I've been thoroughly fucked and left a puddling mess by this man.

Running my fingers through my hair, I take a deep breath and release it slowly. My heart threatens to thump out of my chest with adrenaline.

How amazing. The sex is unreal. I've *never* been able to come so hard, so quickly—my limbs are still quivering. My deepest darkest fantasies are coming to life with a perfect stranger. Well, I wouldn't say Phoenix is a stranger now, but I don't even know what he looks like. All I know is that he's inside my head and owns my body. I'm ruined for anyone else now.

I've never felt so alive.

I know it's unfair to put that on a stranger, but he's intoxicated me with the softest kiss and the slightest touch. He's the intoxication that shuts a soul down and then wakes it into something more powerful.

After a moment, my heart calms down to a slight flutter. With that, I straighten my clothes, run my fingers through my hair again, and find my way back to the path.

"Marco?" I try.

"Polo!" Evie shouts from somewhere to my right.

My shoe hits a broken stalk and sends me stumbling forward. I manage to catch my balance before I face-plant. "Marco!"

I turn a corner and walk down a way, still not seeing her or the girls.

"Polo!"

I sigh, then spin around and walk in the opposite direction, turning another corner. "Marco?" I strain my ears to listen.

"Polo!"

I round the next corner and see Evie and the girls. *Finally*.

Evie glares at me. "Where have you been?"

"I got lost." I scrunch my nose playfully and look toward the girls. Sophie and Lucy both have a stack of fallen leaves in their hands. Lucy tosses hers up in the air, then scrambles to get out of the way as they fall. Sophie does the same but tries to catch them on the way down.

"You have a leaf . . ." Evie pauses. She tugs on my hair and produces two small leaves.

"You know," I muse, "there's something magical about being surrounded by all this corn."

She gives me a puzzled look before chuckling and shaking her head. "Girl! You didn't!"

I slyly nod. "Oops."

"You dirty woman!"

"Who's dirty?" Sophie asks.

We burst out laughing, but before we can answer, Lucy yells at us.

"Look at this one!" she exclaims, pointing to a pumpkin carved into a grinning cat face.

Apparently, we've come to a clearing adorned with pumpkins of various shapes and sizes arranged in a charming display. Sophie and Lucy rush over to inspect the pumpkins, giggling all the way.

Evie and I follow behind, admiring the craftsmanship of the carvings.

Sophie's eyes light up as she spots another pumpkin with a toothy grin. "And this one looks like it's laughing!"

Evie chuckles. "You two have quite the imagination."

We linger around the pumpkins a little longer before I notice a signpost with arrows pointing in different directions.

"Hey, Evie. Look at this."

She joins me, reading the sign with a grin. "Looks like we've stumbled into a mini adventure within our adventure. Girls, pick one!" She ushers them over.

Lucy and Sophie exchange excited glances once more before pointing in opposite directions, just as they had earlier.

Evie bursts into laughter. "Madi, break the tie."

"Let's go . . . left!"

The girls squeal and jump. Lucy leads the way, and we venture farther into the maze. The corn walls part like a curtain, revealing a path lined with delicate fairy lights and tiny sculptures of woodland creatures. Their gasps and awes fill the air as they walk through the path toward the end of the maze.

"Madi! Fancy running into you here," an irritating voice says behind me. The boxes of frozen pizzas slide around when my cart comes to a screeching halt. *Ugh.*

"It's not like we're not in the same town, you know." I scribble a line through the previous item on my list, focusing on what's next.

Saturday afternoons are typically busy at the grocery store. I try my best to be in and out as efficiently as possible.

Declan walks toward me, taking up more of the aisle than he should with his cart. "What are you doing on this lovely day?"

"Shopping, like most people."

"Let's see . . . Pizza, ice cream, oranges, bananas, and what's this?" A curious grin tugs at his lips. He rifles through my cart and pulls out a box. "Oooh, what do we have here?" He raises an eyebrow in mock surprise.

"Oh, come on. Like you've never seen tampons before." Heat rushes to my cheeks, and I quickly snatch the box out of his hand.

"Sure, but I've never seen them in your cart before." He laughs.

"Very funny, Declan." I shove the tampons back into the cart and pile the pizzas on top of it.

"Stop being such a prude, Maxi Madi."

I snap. "You're an idiot!"

"Hell, I'm willing to bet you're still a virgin. Or did Blake finally hit it and quit it? I haven't seen him around lately."

"Oh, here's your nose back! I found it in my business." Steam blows out of my ears, and I'm gripping the handle of the shopping cart so hard my knuckles are white. That nickname immediately takes me back to a cold morning sophomore year, eight years ago . . .

My book bag was heavy on my shoulder as I struggled to open my locker. I groaned and dropped the bag at my feet, then kicked the locker below mine in frustration. I pulled harder on the door, with no luck.

Declan appeared beside me. "Need some help?"

"Ugh. Yes, please. It won't open." I stepped to the side and let him try.

It took a few tries, but he eventually pried it open. When the door flew open, a dozen maxi pads flew out and scattered all over the floor. His buddies circled us and tossed the pads back and forth.

"Do you really need maxis, Madi?" Declan teased with a smirk. A buddy tossed him a pad, and he held it out to me. "Take it, Maxi Madi."

I snatched it out of his hand, my cheeks burning with embarrassment. Forgetting about my locker and the rest of the pads, I grabbed my bag and ran out of there, tears streaming down my face.

I was the quiet, shy girl. The one who studied on a Friday night, got good grades, had only ever kissed one boy, and never got in trouble. I didn't have tons of friends, but I had a few close ones. It wasn't my fault I'd asked my stepdad to bring me some pads and he grabbed some of my mom's instead of mine . . .

After that, everyone picked up on calling me Maxi Madi. It became my new personal hell. Declan and his buddies called me Maxi Madi for the rest of their time at school, until a year later, when they graduated and he finally left for college. It was only then that the nickname died, for the most part. Even then, I never forgave him for what he did.

Declan brings me back to the present. "Well, shit. Who ate your bowl of sunshine this morning, thunderstorm?" he teases, his voice a blend of velvet and arrogance.

I sigh. "You know, I envy people who have never met you."

"Oh, really? I don't. I'm a fucking ray of happiness!"

Shaking my head, I maneuver my cart around him and head toward the checkout, the rest of my shopping list forgotten. He's ruined a perfectly good Saturday.

Dammit, Declan.

I pop open the trunk in my car, place the groceries inside, and walk around the vehicle to return the cart. When I return to the driver's side, I notice something on the windshield. First, it was the balloons and M&M's. Then, my panties hanging on the mirror. And now, a single red rose sits pinned under the wiper blade.

Chapter Eight

Madi

A WEEK LATER...

The sun dips below the horizon, casting a golden glow over the backyard as I bustle about, adding the finishing touches to the setup for my mom's birthday party. It's not a milestone birthday, but this year has been rough on her, and she could use a little extra celebration.

Every year, I do something special—a tribute to the woman who continuously fills my life with love, laughter, unwavering support, and small lectures when I do something she's not fond of. The air fills with the irresistible scent of freshly baked cookies and honey-baked ham, an interesting combination of flavors.

Nothing but the best for Candace.

I take the last of the rolls and place them on the tablecloth outside, then survey the scene. A satisfied smile settles on my face as I take it in. A long table stands beneath a canopy, twinkle lights twisted around the legs. The tablecloth is cheerful shades of blue with paperweights to hold down the blue and purple balloons. Lanterns dance in the air, swaying in the light breeze.

The timer beside me dings, and I waltz back into the kitchen, then open the oven door and let the scent of freshly baked chocolate-chip cookies hit me in the face. Carefully, I place the cookies on a cooling rack, their edges golden, creating a slight crisp.

Just then, the doorbell rings, and my heart jumps. I brush flour from my hands onto my apron and rush to the front door. Opening the door, my smile widens. My mom's best friend, Sarah, greets me with a warm hug.

"Happy birthday to your mom!" she exclaims, and hands me a gift, her eyes sparkling with enthusiasm.

"Andrew's in the back waiting for Mom." I take the gift and place it on the table in the foyer.

Since it's almost time for the other guests to arrive, I tape a sign on the screen door, telling people to come straight in and head outside. The front door is open and waiting.

I check my watch, grab a fresh pitcher of strawberry lemonade from the kitchen, and head to the backyard, then pour the drink into glasses garnished with lemon and strawberry slices and top them off with two ice cubes. When I turn around, I see Andrew, my stepdad, standing near the canopy, holding a glass of brandy.

My heart swells when I see them together. My mom and Andrew have been a strong, loving presence in my life, their marriage a model of partnership and affection. I approach him, a soft smile tugging at my lips.

"Hey, Andrew."

He turns toward me, his eyes crinkling at the corners when he smiles. "Hi, sweetheart. This looks amazing. You really outdid yourself; your mom is going to love this."

My gaze sweeps over the scene again—the decorations, the mingling guests, the table laden with delicious food—and a sense of satisfaction washes over me. My mom will love this. I recheck my watch and realize she should be pulling into the garage any second.

"Be right back," I say to Andrew, and hustle back into the house.

The garage door opens when I round the corner. "Happy birthday, Mom!" I kiss her cheek and take her briefcase from her.

"Thank you, darling."

"Everyone's outside waiting for you."

She gives me an appreciative smile and nods. "Let me freshen up, and I'll be right out."

A few moments later, we join the rest of the guests outside. Many people have already started eating, their plates plentiful. Mom takes her time going around to each guest and thanks them for being here tonight.

Andrew fills up a plate for Mom and whispers something in her ear. She takes the plate and lightly kisses him. The love that radiates through them is palpable. Her vibrant spirit and Andrew's unwavering support helped shape the woman I am today. The way they look at each other, the way their fingers brush when they pass one another, speaks of a love that only deepens over the years.

Everyone eats and drinks, carrying the conversation into the night. After half an hour, Andrew stands up and clinks a knife against his glass. A quiet hush falls over the backyard.

"Thank you all for joining us tonight," he begins, his voice steady and heartfelt. "As we celebrate Candace's birthday, I can't help but reflect on the incredible journey we've shared together over the past twelve years. From the moment we met, she's brought light, laughter, and boundless love into not only my life, but my son's life too."

All the guests look over at his son, while Andrew only has eyes for my mom. "Every day with her is a gift. Through every challenge and triumph, she stands by my side with support and a heart full of compassion—one I'm not always sure I deserve. Candace, you are the heart and soul of our family, and I am endlessly grateful for your presence in our lives." He raises his glass. "To Candace."

"To Candace," everyone says.

His heartfelt words melt my heart, and my eyes brim with tears as I watch my parents, their connection a source of inspiration for my own relationships and aspirations.

It isn't long before Mom calls for some cake. I slip back into the kitchen and pull the cake from the fridge, the creamy frosting adorned with delicate swirls and colorful sprinkles. Annie from Sweet Apples Bakery was gracious enough to write "Happy Birthday, Candace" in elegant cursive. Taking a step back to close the fridge with my leg, I run into someone, almost knocking the cake out of my hands.

"Hey!" I yell.

Quick hands help me steady the cake. A shock of electricity runs through my body.

"Better be careful, now."

I resist the urge to roll my eyes and smack him. Declan. He always seems to be where I am.

"Maybe you shouldn't sneak up on people carrying large cakes," I huff, and place the cake on the counter.

"Well, maybe you should watch where you're going." He smirks at me.

"Since you're here, would you mind grabbing the candles and the lighter from the shelf?" I ask over my shoulder.

"Sure thing."

I turn around to grab the items but stop short. As he reaches for the top shelf, his shirt rises with the movement. My jaw drops the moment I get a glimpse of a rather large tattoo covering his side and torso—a red and orange phoenix cradling a small white dove.

My insides churn as it fully settles in my brain. I'm going to be sick.

No.

Declan. Phoenix. Little dove.

No, not possible.

My stepbrother is Phoenix—my naughty stalker, my mystery man.

Oh, fuck.

Chapter Nine

Declan

STANDING ON MY TOES, I reach for the candles and lighter, then hand them to her. "There you go."

Madi shoots daggers at me with her glare. Damn, I didn't think I knocked into her *that* hard. She snatches them from me without so much as a *thank you*. Not making eye contact, she turns, adds the candles to the cake, lights them, and then carries the cake to the backyard.

I follow behind her and lead everyone in song. She doesn't join in, her lips forming a straight line.

Andrew clears the spot in front of Candace, and Madi sets the cake down. Candace's smile lights up as she leans in to blow out the candles, friends and family cheering her on. Once the candles are out, Andrew starts cutting the cake. He hands them out, giving his wife the first piece.

Humor dances in my eyes as Madi looks between the three of us. I briefly wonder what's going through her head. Once she realizes everyone is distracted with cake and conversation, she storms toward me and pulls me into the house, then to the mudroom by the garage.

Madi locks the door and turns to me, screeching. "Phoenix? What the fuck, Declan?"

The color drains from my face. I knew she'd find out sooner or later, but I hoped it wouldn't be for a while. I had a few more things planned for her. Do I play dumb or come clean?

"Well?" She stands with her hands on her hips, determined.

"Well, what?" I ask.

"Why did you lie to me?" Hurt laces her voice.

"I didn't lie, my little dove," I taunt. "I withheld the truth. There's a difference."

Her eyes harden as she continues to glare at me. "How could you?"

She takes a step back as I advance toward her. Her eyes never waver from mine, demanding something I'm sure not even she knows. Her wavy hair falls in front of her face when she turns her head.

Playing with the devil inside me, I tuck the fallen piece of hair behind her ear, then cup her cheek. She melts into my grasp but pushes me away just as quickly.

"No. No, we can't do this, Declan."

I take another step forward; she takes another one back. "Tell me you didn't enjoy it."

She looks away. "I didn't." Her chest heaves with her words.

Brushing her hair away from her neck, I say, "The bite mark I left begs to differ." She shudders. "Tell me you're not turned on. Tell me you don't want this. Want me." I reach up again and tuck another piece of hair behind her ear, then back her into the wall behind her. "Tell me you don't want me to kiss your lips and make your pretty little pussy come all over my dick."

"You're despicable," she spits, her cheeks heating to the beautiful pink that looks so good on her.

I cup her face in my hands. "And you're a prude Goody Two-shoes who never does anything she shouldn't, right?"

She huffs. "At least I own it."

"No, you don't. You're hiding." She shakes her head in denial, but I continue. "Those times at the club and the corn maze—those are the real you. Tell me you're not soaking wet for me right now." I lean into her and lightly brush my lips against hers.

A hungry moan releases from my throat when her lips part. I capture them, staking my claim on her. She places a hand on my chest, and for a moment, I think she's going to push me away. Madi takes me by surprise when she fists my shirt instead and pulls me closer, parting her lips, letting my tongue enter. I drink in her breathy moan and swallow it, letting it linger in my soul.

I grip my fingers around her waist, grinding my hard dick against her. My lips continue their assault as she reaches down, undoes my buckle, and unbuttons my pants. Her hand slides into my boxers and firmly grips my shaft. A deep shiver runs through me, her hand feeling even better than I imagined. She moans and starts moving her fist up and down. I grab her tits with both hands and squeeze.

My little dove runs her fingers over the tip of my dick, gathering the bead of precum and smearing it around. "Madi," I breathe, breaking our kiss. My hips buck when she continues moving her hand around me. Her fingers squeeze my length, and I groan.

"Please," she whimpers, and removes her hand.

I smirk at her. "Please, what?"

"Fuck me, Declan."

She pushes down her skirt and panties, slips them off her legs, then waves her panties in front of my face. Oh, she wants to play.

I snatch them and bring them to my nose, inhaling her sweet scent. "Soaking wet. I knew it." Reaching between her legs, I find her slick and ready. I dip a finger into her pussy, and she moans. I shove the panties in her mouth and add another finger. "We don't want Mom and Dad walking in now, do we?"

Her eyes widen with lust, and she clenches around me, but she quickly shakes her head no.

"Goddamn, baby. You're so tight." I lift her leg with my other arm and set her foot on the bench next to us. I watch as her pussy sucks my fingers inside, then add another finger, pumping in and out.

I release a low growl. "You're such a dirty little dove. You like this ... Look at your greedy cunt. It's begging to be fucked, isn't it?" She moans against her panties and bucks her hips. Slowly, I withdraw my fingers, coated in her arousal. I wipe her mess on my dick before lining myself up and sinking into her.

Being inside Madi is the best feeling I've ever had. I'll never get enough.

A loud voice rings out on the other side of the door. "Madi?"

My dad.

We freeze, my dick throbbing inside of her pussy. It's almost impossible to keep still, so I don't—I thrust in and out, inch by inch. Covering her mouth to prevent further noise, I fuck her rough and hard. Her stifled moans still fill my ears, egging me on.

"Honey, she's not back here. Maybe she went upstairs?" he calls to Candace.

Her body shudders against me, and she's coming in my arms. Her arousal drenches my balls. *Holy shit.* My body stills, my dick twitches, and I fill her up with my cum.

"You may not realize it yet, but your body knows exactly who owns it. Doesn't it, my little dove?" I taunt, ready to devour her, to bring her to the edge of every cliff, push her off, and fall alongside her.

Epilogue

Madi

There's something about this man that I can't resist. No matter how hard I fight against my brazen impulses, I find myself falling for him. I want his clever, cruel mouth on my breasts, the head of his cock right at my entrance, teasing me before slowly sliding to the hilt and fucking me like there's no tomorrow.

Declan touches my insides on another level. All he has to do is look at me with a smoldering gaze, and I quiver all over again. And my God, that voice. It's deliciously deep and vibrates through my very soul.

Falling in love with someone is easy; admitting it to yourself and others is the hardest part. Especially when he's your stepbrother.

"You're insatiable." Declan smiles. "And I love that about you."

I bite my lip, nodding, and flutter my eyelashes. "I believe you started this." His length pulses in my fist. I tighten my grip and pump my hand up and down. He stops typing, using both of his hands to cup my face.

"Damn right, I did. How else was I supposed to make you see you belong to me?" Something wicked flashes in his eyes as he leans forward to kiss me like he worships me. And he does.

Declan brings out the best in me. I've never felt so naughty, so filthy, so cherished as I do when I'm with him. His lips brush against my neck, lightly nipping at the skin.

His phone rings, startling us both. "Argh, hang on a second," he says, before picking up the phone.

Patience is not something I'm good at with him. While he brings out the best in me, he also brings out the beast in me.

Moving quickly, I pull my hair back into a ponytail and rise up on my knees. When he gives me a puzzled look, I flash him a daring smile. I lick my lips before sticking my tongue out and running it down his length. He hisses, and my pussy grows slick. Swirling his tip around my tongue, I moan into him, then take more of him into my mouth. I bob my head up and down, taking as much of him as possible.

Voices chatter in the background, a small beep resounds, and then Declan speaks. "I only have so much self-control, little dove."

My lips curl into a sly smile as I glance up to see wild passion written on his face. His eyes are dark and threatening, his knuckles white as he grips the chair.

I hum against his cock in response.

"Oh, you want that, don't you?" He bucks his hips, placing a hand on the top of my head. "Don't say I didn't warn you."

Closing my eyes, I work my mouth and tongue around him, relishing with pride when he groans. When I take all of him in, he pushes down on my head and holds me still. The tip of his cock slides down my throat, causing me to gag around him. He forces his fingers through my hair, pulling tight and then raising my head up before pushing it back down to meet his thrust.

I gag again, saliva dripping down my chin to his balls. He holds my head down and wickedly moves his hips, fucking my mouth. There's no warning before his cum fills my mouth, some of it sliding down my throat, some of it collecting on the sides of my cheeks.

He lifts me off him, panting, his nostrils flaring, eyes wide as he grips my jaw. "Open."

My lips part, his cum seeping between my teeth and gums, some of it dripping down my chin. Without taking his eyes off me, he picks up the phone and says, "Let me call you back," then hangs up the phone.

"You're such a dirty little thing," he groans, collecting the cum on my face with his fingers. "Lick it."

When I lean forward to capture his finger, his other hand slides under my skirt and finds me dripping wet. No panties today, just the way he likes it. He grazes my clit before moving lower to where I want him the most. I swirl my tongue around his fingers, and he pushes them in my mouth as he fucks me with his other hand.

Tears sting my eyes from his delicious assault on my mouth and pussy. He slows his movements before pulling out of me entirely. A needy whine falls from my lips but quiets when he helps me stand.

Declan captures my mouth in a forceful kiss and lifts me onto his desk, sliding my ass to the edge. I wrap my arms around his neck and deepen the kiss. He flips up my skirt and spreads my legs open.

He dips his fingers into my pussy again and pumps them a few times. My breath catches in my throat, and I break our kiss, panting with need. I lean back on his desk, gripping the outer edge.

"Oh, fuck . . ." I moan.

When he adds a fourth finger, my body starts shivering. I need more. Harder. Faster. Rougher. *More.*

As if Declan can read my mind, he wraps his other hand around my throat and grips it tightly. Stars dance around my vision and become brighter when he presses his thumb into my clit, fucking me with his fingers.

"Yes, that's it." His voice surrounds me, and it's all I can do not to melt into a puddle at his feet.

He knows I'm close, because he tightens his grip a little more, pushes his fingers a little farther, and presses on that little button inside of me—the one only he's been able to reach. His fingers pulse and move inside me while he towers over me, capturing my lips in an orgasmic, breathless kiss. My choked moans fall into his mouth, and he accepts them, demanding more.

Declan tightens his grip a little more, and that's all I need to fly off the edge. My body convulses in his touch into an earth-shattering orgasm.

"Goddamn, little dove. Your needy cunt drenched me. You look so beautiful with my fingers in your pussy and my hand around your throat. But you'll look even more beautiful when I take your ass later, baby."

My heart sings with his filthy words. I'll never get tired of hearing them.

The End

Thanks for reading Naughty Stalker! Did you enjoy reading the sexy Halloween story? Please consider leaving a review on Amazon and Goodreads!
Love little holiday snacks? Check out a spicy excerpt from Naughty Doctor, available now.

Quote

Lucy: I was clearing out the desk, and I found this.
Ricky: Why, it's our marriage license.
Lucy: Yeah.
Ricky: Well, what's the matter? Don't tell me it's
expired!

I Love Lucy - Season 1 Episode 26

Naughty Stalker Playlist

Move Your Body by My Darkest Days

Poison Apple by Echo Black

Haunt by Neffex

New Reality by The Word Alive

Bad Things by I Prevail

You Put A Spell On Me by Austin Giorgio

They Don't Know About Us by One Direction

Regrets by Stevie Howie

Go Head by Lenny Cooper

Pray by Xana

Madi and Declan's Recipe

Strawberry Lemonade

Ingredients:

¾ cup of fresh lemon juice*

8 tablespoons of granulated sugar

2 cups of fresh strawberries, plus extra for garnish

4 ½ cups of sparkling water**

Ice cubes (optional)

Instructions:

1. Juice the lemons. Add the lemon juice and sugar to a bowl. Whisk together until the sugar dissolves.

2. Wash and cut the tops off the strawberries, then

add them to a food processor or blender. Puree until completely smooth. Run the strawberry puree through a fine mesh strainer.

3. Next, pour the strawberry puree into a pitcher. Add in the lemon juice and stir.

4. Add in the water and stir to combine. Taste and adjust the flavors if necessary.***

5. Add ice to the serving glasses, if desired, and fill each glass with lemonade.

6. Serve with a strawberry garnish.

Notes:

* Use about 6-7 lemons, depending on the size.

** Plain water or club soda can be substituted for the sparkling water.

*** Add a little more sugar or lemon juice if needed.

Additional note: you can swap the sugar with any sweetener you prefer.

Naughty Doctor Excerpt

Connor

IMAGES OF LEIGH PLAGUE my thoughts. The way her hair cascades down her back. The way her smile makes any room brighter. Her plump pink lips and the way they turn up when she's lost in thought. Her long legs and how they would feel wrapped around my waist. How her pussy tastes, and how much I want to sink my cock into her. These are not images I should be thinking about. I'm her boss.

She surprised me when she asked about someone special in my life. Over the past two weeks, we've shared moments where something could happen. Sadly, they're fleeting, making me wonder if they're one-sided.

I'm her boss. Nothing should happen between us. Nothing can happen between us.

Still, my gaze lingers on her body longer than a boss's gaze should. My body responds in a way a boss's shouldn't. I know she feels it too, even though she won't say it.

This pull between us. It's electric. Tantalizing.

Her fingers graze my arm when she passes me in the hallway. The glances are flirty, but coupled with a wicked smile, my insides turn into Jell-O. She teases me when she stretches her legs under the counter as if daring me to look. Her clothes cling to her every curve—curves begging to be touched. She rakes her eyes up and down my body, wanting me as much as I crave her.

"Good morning, Dr. Wilson," she greets me. Leigh walks around the counter, sets her purse down, and removes her coat. She's wearing a graphic T-shirt with Christmas lights and white letters that say "Light It Up," paired with skinny jeans and a pair of snow boots. I forgot today's casual Friday.

I shift my position and discreetly adjust the instant hard-on in my pants. "Good morning, Leigh." *I'm her boss.*

She crinkles her nose and flashes me a smile. "It's going to be a good day today. There's something in the air. I can feel it." Cute green Christmas trees hang from her earlobes, reminding me of the mistletoe I have in my office. I make a mental note to stick it in my pocket for later.

"Yes, it will be," I say, and give her a knowing look. She doesn't know yet just how good today will be. With that, I head into my office in the back and bury myself in my notes before patients start arriving.

A few moments later, Leigh knocks on the door.

"Dr. Wilson?"

"Leigh." I motion for her to come in. "What can I do for you?"

"Mrs. Johnson is here for your nine o'clock."

"Got it. I'll be right out." She steps out of the office, but I'm quick behind her.

"Leigh," I breathe.

She turns around, bumping straight into me. "Oops, sorry." I reach out to catch her, wrapping my arm around her waist before she loses her balance. Her gaze meets mine, heating my insides as I read her expression. Cheeks red, breaths heavy. She's not sorry. Not even a little bit.

"You forgot something."

"Oh, did I?" she asks, innocently looking from side to side.

"Up here?" I tease, wiggling the mistletoe above our heads. Leigh lets out a gasp as I pull her closer. "You forgot to give me a kiss this morning."

She giggles. "A little presumptuous, isn't it?" However, her body tells a different story. Her chest rises and falls quickly, and she leans her head closer, her gaze flicking between my eyes and my mouth.

My lips curl up in a cocky smirk. "No. You'll kiss me by the end of the day." I tilt my head down to meet hers, our lips almost touching. I breathe her in and bask in her peppermint scent, the remnants of the candy cane she was undoubtedly sucking on moments earlier.

Leigh lifts her hand and traces along my jaw. "Maybe in your dreams. You've got a patient, doc." She slips out of my grip and saunters down the hallway, tossing me a glance over her shoulder before she turns the corner.

Fuck me.

It isn't until noon that I find myself alone with her. Her back is facing me as she stands in the break room, and I take a moment to enjoy her ass in those jeans. It jiggles as she taps her foot in sync with the song playing throughout the office. The microwave in front of her beeps, and she opens it, grabs her mug, and sets it on the counter. She reaches for the napkins and uses one to pick up two of the Christmas cookies Annie brought by this morning.

In three long strides, I capture my little mouse in front of me by placing my hands on both sides of her and caging her in against the counter. Her body stiffens against me. Then, leaning forward so my mouth is right beside her ear, I whisper, "Your lips on mine will be the best Christmas gift this year."

Some of the tension melts from her body as she cocks her head to the side. "Oh. I thought me tied in a bright red bow would be the best thing?"

A strand of hair falls in front of her face. I smooth it behind her ear, then gently graze her neck with my lips. She gasps at the contact and arches her back, leaning into my chest. My cock is hard and straining against the small of her back. It's all I can do not to grind into her.

"Playing with fire gets you burned, little mouse." I trail my tongue down her neck to her shoulder, then tug on her sleeve, revealing more skin and a small tattoo—a dark red heart with horns. A shiver rips through her as I nip her shoulder.

This will be fun.

The thought is fleeting, as Leigh twists away from me with a smirk. "You have no idea, boss." She winks, grabs her cookies and what smells like apple cider, then walks back toward the front of the office.

Still facing the counter, I palm my cock to release some tension. Unfortunately, it only makes me harder. And just when I think it can't get any worse, it does.

Acknowledgements

Gwen: thank you for being my hype woman. These holiday snacks are for you! I promise more are coming.

Chris: you're the best I could've asked for. I love you. Thank you.

Elle: the cover is stunning! I absolutely love it. You've made the vision come alive.

Rachelle: I can never thank you enough for your outstanding edits. The formats look so good too! You truly are amazing.

Dee: I love your editing tips and questions. You always find something extra for me to think about.

Read more from Zoey Zane

Out Now

a beautiful broken life
He Calls Me Bug
(previously in Cheaters: A Dark Romance Anthology)
Countdown Madness
Naughty Doctor
Unwrapping Spring Break
She Calls Me Daddy
Naughty Stalker

Coming Soon

Naughty Planner
Sweet Like Sugar, Thick Like Honey

Meet Zoey

ZOEY ZANE IS AN author and poet, but will always be a zealous reader at heart. She has a love for dark romance and thrillers, the two genres that dominate most of the space on her bookshelves. Zoey lives in Tennessee with her husband, their son, and their two adorable pit bulls.

You can find me at zoeyzane.net, by scanning the QR code, or on the sites below!

a amazon.com/Zoey-Zane/e/B08K56BJZ2/

f facebook.com/zoeyzaneauthor

BB bookbub.com/authors/zoey-zane

g goodreads.com/author/show/20671544.Zoey_Zane

⊙ instagram.com/justmekendra/